WICKED INK CHRONICLES

SHATTERED
ink

NEW YORK TIMES BESTSELLING AUTHOR
LAURA WRIGHT

Addison

"You're kidding me with all this, right?" Lisa asks, her pointer finger tracing an imaginary Z down my body.

"All what?" I ask with slight irritation.

Lisa's crystal blue eyes, expertly rimmed in charcoal, narrow. "The toddler-napwear-meets-prison-inmate thing you're working."

The ocean breeze kicks my hair around my face. "Orange is the new black, Lis."

She looks insulted. "That's insane. Who said that?"

"I don't know. I think I heard it on Colbert last week."

"Colbert is a comedy show, Addy."

Tired, and not up for the night out my best friend has dragged me to once again, I take a step back, lift my arms. "Look, I see nothing wrong here. Just, you know, trying to be comfortable on a Thursday night."

"You look like you're headed to bed."

"I wish I was," I return with a bit of a pout, then silently amend, to *Rush's* bed. His big bed, cool sheets, and that hot, hot body I miss so much it hurts. I groan.

"You're losing it, Addy. You know that, right?"

I frown at her, but inside my mind I'm screaming YEAH, I DO.

Growing more exasperated with me by the minute, Lisa glances over her shoulder at the dozens of people coming in and out of the large Santa

Barbara oceanfront house, spotlighted in moonglow and about thirty iPhone screens. I can practically feel her urgency to get in there, mix it up, flirt her sexy leather ass off with all the boys she's been crushing on at school. But I'm keeping her from it. With my orange sweatpants and tear-stained t-shirt.

When she turns back, she looks mutinous. "I'm just going to say one thing to you: Vegas."

My insides go instantly hot and soft. It's a depressing feeling, but addicting and predictable. Kind of like my life has been over the past five weeks. When Rush and I chucked the past and decided to try this again, I was so happy. So excited. A second chance at a first love. But as Lisa put it, I'm losing it. In the past five weeks, I've only seen him three times, and for no more than a day or two. I have school and finals and graduation, and he

3

LAURA WRIGHT

has work and travel. It's like the most beautiful torture in the world, seeing him. I'm on a high when I'm around him. When he's gone, I crash. And I can't seem to bounce back. I'm utterly and completely addicted to him. I'm jealous of anything and anyone who gets to be near him, and there are actually times when I don't give a shit about graduating, about getting my marketing degree—about a job or a future. I just want to be in his atmosphere. I just want those eyes locked on mine, and those inked arms around me.

Of course, I haven't told him any of this. I don't want him to think I'm a loser. I don't want him to know the truth. I don't want him to walk away from me—or shit, run—because this time, it's not just love that would be lost. It'd be my heart, my breath…my sanity.

SHATTERED
ink

"Vegas, Addy," Lisa repeats, her perfectly arched brows lifting expectantly. "You owe me."

I sigh, at her, at myself and my crazy thoughts, and stuff my hands in the pockets of my orange sweatpants. "Come on, Lis. I paid you back for the convention a million times. Don't make me remind you—or myself—about that waxing party I helped you host."

Her mouth twitches. "No, sister friend. This isn't payback for the convention. This is for all the drives back and forth to the airport, the hours of listening to Rush's messages and trying to decode what he's *really* saying, the mornings I pull your ass out of bed and to class."

I actually recoil. "Seriously?"

"Hells yeah, seriously."

5

Some random guy walks by and gives Lisa a very dazzling, very appreciative smile. I don't blame him. She looks hella sexy in her tight leather pencil pants, low-cut lacy top and messy side braid. As she returns the smile, her expression curling into one of heat and promises, she waves at him. For second, I remember what it's like to flirt casually and just have a good time—act my age—and I don't miss it. Any of it. I only miss him.

I inhale deep and exhale heavy. God, this is bad. I shouldn't be this obsessed, this close to the edge, over a guy. I know Rush isn't feeling this way. Or at least he doesn't act like it. When we talk or see each other, he's chill, sexy, into me, for sure. But not like this—not like me.

When Lisa turns back to face me, takes in my relaxed-wear once again, she sighs. "Look. I know

you miss him, Addy. I know you're head over heels, as the kids say. I know you want to be with him every second of the day. But you're starting to fall apart."

"Starting?" I say on a slightly manic laugh.

Lisa remains serious. "It's so not like you."

"I know." I shake my head. "I've never felt like this, Lis. Sometimes it's actually hard to breathe. It's more than just loving him, it's the fear of losing him. Just the thought of it breaks me apart inside. I don't know what to do with that."

Her expression softens. "I get it. I do. But you're going to have to hold back and chill out. What you're working here isn't cute, if you know what I mean. I believe the boys call it Psycho Bitch."

"Nice." But I know she's right.

"Maybe you need to take a little break from each other?"

"No." The word is out of my mouth fast and impassioned.

"Date other people?"

"Impossible."

Lisa's lips press together in a worried frown. For a second, she just stares at me. Then she shrugs. "Okay."

I know that word, *and* that look. She's freaked out by me. *Welcome to the club, sister friend.* "I'm sorry."

She shakes her head.

"No, seriously," I continue. "I'm sorry I'm such a mess. I'm sorry I'm being such a shit-tastic friend."

"Don't worry about it. I love my little train wreck in orange." A smile tugs at her lips.

I'm surprised when my mouth curves upward. "Okay. So, let's forget about my insanity and obsessive needs for a few hours. We're going to party. Hard. Loose. Wild."

She laughs. "Oh, Jesus."

"And." I gesture to my offending ensemble. "Just to show you I'm trying, I'll go home and change."

Lisa shakes her head. "No, you're fine. Actually, maybe it's better this way. Dolled up, you bring competition to the field, and you know I'm good with getting all the attention. Come on, beeyotch." She grabs my hand and leads me through and around several small pockets of students and up the path to the front door. "And for the record, fashion-wise, orange isn't the new

anything. Except maybe a huge boner killer."

RUSH

"There's a rule about this, bro."

"Yup," I say, staring at the top of Vincent's head, which is now sporting a green-tipped mohawk. The guy is worse than a chick when it comes to style and color up top.

"And I think you're the knucklehead who came up with it," he continues.

I mentally shrug. "Could be."

Vincent pulls back on the iron and flips his peepers up to meet mine. I notice he's added a second piercing to his eyebrow. "So, what gives, man? And don't tell me it's the *looooovvvve* that's brought your ass to my chair—because I've seen you turn away rock royalty when they wanted the name of some chick inked onto their skin."

Discussing my private shit with anyone makes my balls shrink, so I point at my hand, aka V's work in progress. "Can you finish?"

"I just don't get it, bro," he continues like the deaf numbnuts he is. "Breaking the rules for a hot piece of ass has never been your—"

My eyebrows jack up and I send him a look. "Hey. Watch yourself."

"What?"

"You don't talk like that. You know, not if you want to keep your blood inside your body and all."

"Shit, bro. So hostile."

"Addison's my girl, dickhead," I growl. "Not a hot piece of ass."

"I dunno, man." Vincent starts back in on me, moving up my thumb with his signature shade of black. "Addison has a pretty hot ass. I mean, I've never seen it without denim or anything, but I can imagine—"

"I swear to motherfucking god—" I start between teeth so tightly clenched my jaw protests.

Vincent chuckles. "Don't move. Or this 'I' is going to be busted. Damn, she has a long name. Good thing you got the room. Big hands." His mouth curls into a Hollywood grin. "Addison likes that, I bet."

The urge to send the heel of my boot into his junk is crazy strong. But you know, I don't want to bleed out from the needle he's using on me. Not when I'm going to see my baby tomorrow. "I think I need to fire your ass when we're done here."

"That what you think?" He laughs. "Shit, Merrick. You know you need me. Besides my obvious skills with an iron, I'm the only testosterone you got around here."

It's my turn to laugh. "Get serious, man. Janie's got more T than the both of us combined."

He grunts. "Heh, heh. True that."

Just sitting in the guy's dungeon-inspired room, watching him do his thing, that motherfucking perfect line work, I close up shop on the banter that just ends in me wanting to knock him into Sunday, and go silent for awhile. Which I guess opens me up to thoughts I've been trying to tamp down lately. Like maybe why it is I've broken my rule. The rule that states crystal fucking clear: No Names Inked Onto Skin. I mean, shit…it's like the kiss of death. Total jinx. An omen. A relationship killer. In my

biz, I've seen it a hundred times. So what am I doing? Testing? Teasing? Seeing how strong we got it?

Or maybe…fuck me…maybe I want her to know how deep it runs for her, you know? Like she's in my goddamn blood. She's mine. Maybe I want her to see it tomorrow and say to me, *Baby, put your name on my body, too. Somewhere real visible. Because I want every guy who takes a look and thinks he's got a chance with me to think again.*

"All right, idiot," Vincent says, setting his iron down and mopping me up. "You're done. She's on you forever. So basically you got a week or two before this thing crashes and burns."

"Dick." I look down at my thumb. Her name scripted in black. My eyes follow the lines, from A to N, and my dick goes hard. I close my eyes and

15

breathe deep. The tent popping isn't something I want V to witness. Dude has zero filter, and I'm kinda itching to knock him in the back of the head.

"Your girl coming this weekend?" Vincent asks me, spreading some goop over Addison's name.

Coming? Fuck yeah she is. Over and over until she's hoarse, and my neighbors a mile away call to complain. But I know that ain't what V means, so I just nod.

"You bringing her to the shop?" he asks as he wraps up my thumb.

"Course." I'm bringing her everywhere with me. Stuck to my side and my front and my mouth like super glue. It's been ten days since I've touched her. And guess what? I know how many hours and minutes it's been too—I'm just not that big of a douche to acknowledge it out loud.

"When?" V asks, ripping off his gloves and pushing back toward the trash can in his roller chair.

I shrug. "I don't know."

"Friday night?"

"No, not tomorrow night." My whole body gets kind of hot and bothered. Tomorrow night is my night to ask her the big question. Tomorrow night's the night I tell her she's gonna move in with me after grad. That she's gonna move to Vegas permanently, and let me take care of her because, fuck, I can't keep waking up without her. And I sure as hell can't keep imagining her back in Cali, looking all sweet and sexy, getting hit on by a bunch of beach ballers—especially those *vanilla* beach ballers.

"What about Saturday?" Vincent continues. "She coming in Saturday?"

"Okay, what the fuck is this about?" I stand up and give him a quick sneer. "You crushing on my girl or is this about that Lisa chick?"

V goes kinda red, which makes me snicker a little in spite of my irritation with him.

He turns away, shrugs. "Don't know anyone named Lisa, man."

I laugh. "You ever gonna tell me what happened there?"

"Don't know what you're yammering about, brother, and don't want to."

Fine. I don't need to know. As long as it doesn't involve Addison, I don't give a shit what or who V does. "Then why do you keep pressing me about bringing my girl into the shop?"

Vincent turns back, the red face thing gone. He's got one of those shit-eating grins the ladies

seem to like, but I don't get it. "I just want to witness the meet and greet, that's all."

"Okay, Riddler, I'm so glad you didn't ink my fuck off finger." I flip him off.

"You forgot, didn't you?" When I stare blankly at him, he chuckles. "Oh, you stupid bastard."

I flip him off again and head for the door. "Thanks for the ink, asswipe."

"Our guest, Rush," he calls after me. "Or technically, your guest."

A foot from the door, I slow up. My brows slam together and I glance over my shoulder. Vincent is leaning back in his chair, hands behind his head, showing off his most prized possession, his Banksy t-shirt.

"Wicked Ink welcomes Erica Day this weekend," he says. "That ring a bell?"

My cock twitches and not because it's excited.

How the hell hadn't I remembered this? "Fuck."

Vincent flashes me the pearlies, his black eyes going all wicked jackass-ness. "The old girlfriend gets to meet the new girlfriend.

Addison

"I so totally failed my Econ final," I tell Lisa as we head into the Santa Barbara airport, which is pretty light on the customers for a Friday afternoon. "That's what I get for the hard partying last night."

She snorts while pulling her white blond hair into a messy bun. "Dudette, you didn't even drink."

"And yet I feel hung over."

She laughs. "At least you're not wearing your sad girl clothes any longer."

"Don't hate, beeyotch," I faux scold as we head for one of the available Check-In kiosks. "And you know what? I actually got hit on last night. Even in my orange sweats and tear-stained t-shirt."

Her mouth drops one. "Wait. Some horny frat boy smelled the desperation on you and went for it? I refuse to believe it."

I shake my head. "So mean."

She blows me an air kiss. "It's why you love me."

"No," I say, laughing. "That's not why." I type in the confirmation code Rush emailed me yesterday. Since I'm always going to him, he insists on paying for my flights. I feel weird about it, even tried arguing with him about it, but it's no use. When Rush Merrick wants something, he gets it.

A shiver moves through my body at the thought, and everything below my waist gets all tight and hot. Oh yeah, I miss him.

SHATTERED
ink

"Hey," Lisa says, snapping her fingers near the touch screen. "Confirm your flight so I can get out of here, girlie. I gots some serious plans."

She draws out that last word which is usually code for 'I'm not thrilled about this, but I'm doing it anyway,' and after OKing my flight and setting the thing to print my boarding pass, I turn to look at her. "Guy from last night or somebody new?"

She snorts. "I wish it was the guy from last night." Her eyes lose a little of their mischievous blue glow. "It's someone my family set me up with. Real Santa Barbara blue blood, buttoned up, junior partner in my dad's law firm kind of thing."

"Sorry, Lis. I know how much you hate buttons."

"It's fine." She shakes her head, trying to play off like it's no big deal when we both know the control her family has over her and her future makes her insane.

"It's one date," I say, adding a casual shrug for good measure.

"I know." She takes a deep breath and gives me a forced smile. "Okay. Go see your beautiful tattooed man, fuck his brains out, tell him you love him a hundred times then come back and finish your last week with a clear head, okay?"

"Yeah, okay."

Sensing my hesitation, her perfectly manicured brows draw together. "What?"

"Graduation is next weekend."

"Right."

"So, I'm just thinking, what then, you know? Where do we go? Do we stay in California? Do I

stay in California? Do I find a job here? Or…do I

go to Vegas?"

Lisa blinks, slightly confused. "Oh. Well,

Vegas I guess. Right?"

I shrug. "I don't know."

She chews her lip, maybe deciding what she

should say. "What's Rush say?"

Rush…he's said nothing. He hasn't even

mentioned it. "We haven't talked about it. I don't

even know if he's coming to graduation."

"So ask him."

I study the floor of the airport for a second.

"Maybe."

"Come on, Addy, the guy loves you."

"I know." I grab my boarding pass and try to

kill the conversion by looking anywhere but at Lisa.

She doesn't go for it. "Okay. What are you thinking?"

My eyes can't help themselves. They connect with hers again. "What if he's having second thoughts? What if he's not that into me anymore? What if what happened between us five weeks ago was just leftover sparks that needed to be released?"

Lisa stares at me like I'm nuts. "Jeez, no wonder you failed your final."

"Right?" I return with a pathetic laugh. "I need to back off a little, don't I? Stop putting so much pressure on us? Play it cool before I lose him to my madness. I don't want that to happen again. Besides you, he's the only family I got."

Before Lisa can answer, the customer service rep comes over to check my ticket. "Any bags?"

I hold up my carry-on. "Just this."

"Enjoy your flight," the woman says coolly before walking away.

"First Class again," Lisa says.

I glance over at her. She's stolen my boarding pass and is looking over it with her x-ray vision. "Every time. The boy's got skills, that's for sure." She hands it back to me. "Listen, girlie, I don't blame you for holding on tight and getting freaked out when you think he's not. After how you grew up, it's understandable. Probably to Rush, too. But may I suggest, instead of playing, maybe you should just be honest with him."

I release a heavy breath. "So show him my crazy? You said it yourself, psycho bitch isn't sexy."

"Come here." Lisa gives me a hug. "I love you, mama."

27

"Love you, too."

"See you tomorrow night?"

I nod against her shoulder. "You know, Lis, I can totally take a cab—"

She pulls back and gives me her fiercest mock glare. "Don't make a beeyotch cut you."

"You're not a beeyotch. You're a whore." I smile broadly. "I better go. Text me about your date, 'k?"

Her fierce expression fades a touch, but she rallies and tosses me a kiss and a quick wave before heading for the door. I guess we both have our issues to deal with.

I turn and make a beeline for security. In a few hours, I'm going to see Rush. And in turn, he's going to see me. But the calm-cool-collected-and-completely-unconcerned-about-the-future me. Not

the crazy chick who feels like her world is falling

apart when she's not around him.

RUSH

Something's doing in my gut as I stand outside the Vegas airport in the slowly diminishing sunlight and watch Addison's plane come in for a landing. It's like a dozen furry little creatures are running around in there, banging up against shit. It's not a totally unfamiliar feeling. It usually happens right before I see my girl. Along with the twitchy hands dance, and the cotton mouth bullshit. Yeah, that's right, my body misses hers something deep and awful. It couldn't give a shit about all the sex text and phone fondling we do. It wants her soft heat right up on it or it's just not happy.

The plane lands nice and safe, and with a stupid-ass grin attached to my face, I head inside the terminal and go wait in my regular spot at baggage claim. She knows the spot real well. Will be expecting to see me there. Though today I got a little surprise up my sleeve. Or in my pocket.

I roll my eyes. Don't know if it's douche-like or romantic, but maybe I got a small piece of white paper with her name on it in my back pocket. And maybe I'm gonna take it out and hold it up above my head like a goof when she starts my way. And then, maybe, when she sees it—and me—she'll come running. She'll run at me and jump on me, wrap her sexy, long legs around my waist and just hold on tight. Hold on forever. And, fuck, as her ankles cross right above my ass, her mouth'll cover mine and make me happy to be alive again, make the crazy in my belly recede.

Someone barks out something on the loudspeaker, and a few yards away the carousel conveyor belt kicks into gear and starts spitting out luggage. My peepers jack around, looking for her. That beautiful long brown hair and those mismatched eyes, all housed in the hottest, tightest, tastiest body on the planet.

It's only about five minutes later that I spot her, behind a guy in a business suit and a couple who are clearly jazzed to get hitched by Elvis. Like a teenager in heat, my heart drops south and my dick starts to swell. I never realize just how badly I miss her until I see her face.

I reach around, fumble into my pocket and grab the paper, lift it above my head. It's nothing much. Just some notebook scrap. But I want her to know how nuts I am to have her here. Back with me. Shit…home.

Dressed in jeans and a bright pink tank, her hair loose around her shoulders, she looks hot, as drop dead gorgeous as the motherfucking sunset outside, and I can't wait to have her in my arms. But as she gets closer, I also see how tired she looks. Bone weary, as the songs say. Or is it stressed? I can't tell. I push away from the wall I've been holding up and curse. I hate it. Want to wring its neck. Whatever it is that's made her this way. School, me, late nights, parties—I stop myself right there. I stop myself because my gut is going tight. Like pissed, jealous, controlling-dude tight, and I don't like that guy. He's weak and an embarrassment to all who have dicks.

The couple headed for Elvis and wedded bliss take off to the right, and Addison's gaze shifts to the very spot I'm standing in, her eyes instantly locking with mine. She stops inside the very center of the departing crowd, her face and her expression completely unreadable to me. It's not her usual look, and something ice cold moves down my spine. I remember that she was quiet this morning on the phone, kinda distant. I'd chalked it up to nerves. She'd been rushing off to her econ final. But maybe I was wrong. Maybe there was something more to it.

Slowly, her gaze travels up my heavily inked arms to my face, to the scrap of paper above my head. She blinks for a second, staring at it. Then like the goddamn sun ripping out from behind the clouds, she smiles—so wide and so bright, I fucking die from relief. I'm about to slip the paper back in my pocket and jog over to her, grab her bag and haul her into my arms, kiss the shit out of her for about ten minutes, when she drops the black leather duffle at her feet and takes off toward me.

Around us, shit is happening, people are staring, that chick on the loudspeaker is announcing something. But we don't care. I don't care. Nothing exists except me and her. It's always been that way with us. And I'm starting to believe it's both our strength and our vulnerability.

"Rush!" She barrels into me, her arms going around my waist, her cheek hitting my chest.

But I got to see her, need to see those eyes, one blue, and the green one that belongs to me, up close and personal. I gotta see that she's okay, that the stress I noticed earlier isn't about me or us. My

hands plunge into her hair, one curling around to cup her neck. With a whimper, her head drops back and she stares up at me with a look so frantic and hungry and lust-filled I'm thinking it's a mirror to my own.

"Oh fuck, baby, I missed you," I manage to get out before I drop my head and feast on her.

Addison

I'm lost. In him. In his tongue and his teeth, his mouth and his breath, and the way he whispers my name between every kiss as we practically stumble out of the airport and over to where he's parked his bike.

I know we've got to separate at some point to get out of here, get home, but my entire body's on fire, screaming at me to find a dark corner and just unzip.

I feel cool metal against my hand as Rush rips his mouth from mine. We must be here. In the parking garage. And hey, there are lots of dark corners. But before I can suggest it, Rush lifts me up with a growl and places me on the black leather seat. Breathing heavy, my lips already deliciously swollen, I watch as he straps my bag onto the back of the bike. Every inch of my skin is vibrating and I'm squeezing the black leather with my inner thighs. I've never felt so manic. Like if I don't get my hands on him soon, feel his hot, hard, inked skin against mine, I'll lose my sanity.

So much for my plan to keep it cool.

"Stop looking at me like that, Addison," Rush warns, grabbing his helmet.

I smile innocently. "Like what?"

His green eyes liquid fire, he leans in, close to my ear. "I can't fuck you here. Too many people. Too many cameras." He licks the shell of my ear and I shiver deliciously. "And no one sees you come but me. So, sit tight, baby. I'm taking you home."

He slips the helmet over my head, then climbs on in front of me. For just a second, I take him in. My badass boy with the combat boots, ripped jeans, faded black t-shirt, oh-so sexy disheveled hair and plentiful ink. That beautiful ink I dream about every night. That ink wrapped around my body. I shiver again. All the way down to my toes.

"Arms around me, baby," Rush calls, starting the engine.

He gives me less than a few seconds to do as he says before ripping away from the space and hauling ass out of the parking structure. He's such a skilled maniac, the way he takes every curve and slides in and out of lanes. I love it. I get off on it.

We're just merging onto the freeway when my insides calm down enough to enjoy the ride and the desert wind on my skin. Shit, could I move here?

Live in Las Vegas, in the desert, with him? Yes, I could. I know that. I want that. But does he? Does he understand that if we did that, things would be crazy for awhile? That I'd be job searching for weeks, maybe months while I worked temp jobs to pay for an apartment? Because I'd be paying for my own shit. Or…would he fight me on that? Like he fights me on the plane tickets? And if I gave in, would that screw with our dynamic?

I roll my eyes inside my helmet. I'm getting way ahead of myself here. He hasn't asked. He hasn't even mentioned it. Maybe he's content with this…seeing each other when we have time. Flying in and out, weekends when it's cool. Maybe I need to just stop this head trip I'm on and enjoy my time with him.

SHATTERED
ink

Rush takes a hand off the handlebars and places it over mine, which are tightly wrapped around his waist. The move, the contact of his skin on mine, completely unravels me again. And as Rush exits the freeway and hits the two lane road that leads to his house, I inch closer, press my breasts against his back and squeeze my thighs around his hips. I feel him inhale sharply. Around us, the pink sun is going down, and without thinking, my right hand abandons his waist and starts to descend.

"Addison." I hear the warning-laced call on the wind, but I'm barely registering it. I want him so badly I can't see straight.

He groans as my fingers brush lightly over the top of his burgeoning erection. I want it. I want to slip my hand inside his jeans and make him as hard as the red rocks around us.

LAURA WRIGHT

"Baby, I'm going to crash," he hollers back, his voice strained.

I know. I hear him, and I know what he's saying is true. Shit, I know what I'm doing is totally freaking dangerous. But I don't care. I swear to god, I want him so bad I don't care if we crash.

What the hell is wrong with me? And how can I make it stop?

With a hard jerk to the right and a squeal of tires, Rush pulls off the road. I curl into him, holding on tight as he speeds into the desert, hauling ass until he spots a large palo verde tree about quarter mile out. He guns for it, and once there, jerks the bike to the right, then brings it to an abrupt, dust-clouded stop before killing the engine. He's off the thing in two seconds. Has me on my

44

feet in one. And rips off my helmet with a curse and look so fierce, I shiver and erupt into flames.

"That wasn't very smart, Ads," he says, unbuttoning the top of his jeans.

My breath catches in my throat. "I know. I'm sorry."

His mouth twitches, but the humor doesn't reach his eyes. He sends his zipper down a few inches. "No you're not."

"You're right, I'm not," I say as he moves closer until his body is flush against mine. "I want you. I'm not going to apologize for that."

He leans down, kisses my top lip super gently, then bites it.

I hiss and my belly clenches.

"We're not making it home, Ads. Not like this." He reaches for me. Quick and easy, he unbuttons and unzips my jeans, his fingers moving downward. "I'm hard and you're…" He fiercely cups me through my jeans. "Wet."

I groan and push against his hand. Hell yeah, I'm wet. I need him so badly, need him to touch me, put me out of my misery so I can think clearly again.

"I'm going to have to fuck you right here, Ads." His eyes meet mine. "Is that what you want?"

I can barely breathe. "Yes."

One eyebrow lifts. "Anyone could see us."

I shake my head, lick my dry lips. "I don't care."

He grins. "Shit, baby. We could get arrested."

I grin back, my heart slamming against my ribs so hard it's painful. "Then you'd better hurry up and get inside me."

"Oh, that's a great answer." In one effortless move, he flips me around to face the bike, then hooks his thumbs inside of the waistband of my jeans and sends them to my ankles. "Perfect answer."

The cool desert breeze blows across the skin of my legs and ass as he bends me over the leather seat of his bike and kicks my feet apart as far as the denim will allow. I'm dying. Fucking dying to have him inside me. I hold my breath, every inch of me so sensitive that when he does touch me, when he slides my thong aside, when I feel his hand moving down the seam of my ass, then slowly—oh-so erotically slowly—entering me with one long, thick finger, I convulse.

Rush lets out a groan and holds me steady with his free hand. "Oh, baby, you're so wet." He inserts a second finger and drives it up all the way up to the knuckles. "How long have you been like this?"

Breathing heavy, nipples beading, fingers digging into the leather seat, I manage to utter one word. "Hours."

He pumps me slowly. "I don't think I've ever felt you this wet."

"I tried to take care of it on the plane."

"Where?" he demands.

I feel his cock against my ass. It's hard and warm and ready. "The bathroom."

Rush stills, then spreads his fingers wide inside of me, stretching me. It's delicious, and I moan. "Did you touch yourself, Addison?"

"Yes."

He slips his fingers out of me and finds my clit. When he brushes over it with his thumb, I gasp and clench. "Here?"

God, I'm going to die. "Yes."

"Did you stroke yourself? Pinch yourself?"

My nails dig into the leather seat as he does both with his clever fingers. "Yes."

"Did you come?"

I shake my head. I can't breathe or focus.

"Good." The head of his cock is right against my opening now. I arch my back, silently begging him to fill me. "You won't do that again. Got it, Addison? I make you come. Only me."

Without waiting for a response, he pushes inside me. Not all the way, just an inch or two. "Unless I'm watching."

LAURA WRIGHT

My eyes fill with tears. I've never wanted anything so bad in my life. "Rush, please!"

"In fact." He slips in another inch, then two. "When we get home, you're going straight to my room." He pulls out, and I cry and let my head drop forward. "You're going to get naked."

"Yes, yes, please Rush, I can't—"

"You're going to get on my bed." He slams into me, so hard and so deep I gasp for air, grip the bike to hold myself steady. "You're going to spread your legs so wide I can see every inch of you. Then you're going to fuck yourself."

His hands clamp around my hips and he thrusts inside me with deep, wonderfully punishing strokes.

"But right now, baby, I'm fucking you."

My brain is a blank screen, and my throat is only allowing moans and sighs and cries to escape.

50

Under the slowly darkening sky, with the sounds of the wind, and the traffic in the distance, Rush works me over, his hands splayed on my ass now, his thumbs opening my cheeks wide, so he can get inside me even deeper. It's heaven, and I never want it to end. But my body is betraying me. The build started the second I saw him with that sign above his head at the airport, and the cocky grin on his face when he saw me. So when leans over me, gets close to my ear and whispers, "I love you awful, baby," I break. My walls contract around him, my legs shake and I cry out into the night-blooming desert.

Rush curses and squeezes my hips. He stays by my ear as he pounds into me. He whispers my name over and over as he too lets go. It's been so long since we've been together. For a week, our skin, our tongues, our insides have been running on memory and withdrawal. We needed this. Quick and hard and wherever we could find the space.

Rush doesn't linger inside of me. Night's coming on fast now and I'm getting cold. With gentle hands, he pulls my jeans back up, even zips and buttons me, then handles himself before straddling his bike and gesturing for me.

"Get on, Addison. We need to go home." His sexy, jade-green eyes heavy with lust, he revs the engine at me. "That only made me want your ass more."

I don't need to hear anything more. I'm his. Whatever he wants, and whenever he wants it. I yank on my helmet, then settle in behind him, my arms wrapping around his waist. He takes off back toward the road, kicking up desert dust, and I

realize that for the first time in a week, I can finally

breathe right.

RUSH

So we're playing this game, are we? Follow the Leader? Not what I had planned. Not until much later anyway. But shit, I wasn't kidding when I said that quickie back on my bike was a tease.

As I stalk her, passing through the kitchen I see the table all set for dinner. I know there's a kickass meal staying warm in the oven. I know because I ordered it, and told the chef who made it to be gone before I got back. I wanted her alone. Wanted to eat with her alone.

My boot nearly collides with her bra. It's the bright pink one, no lace, all satin, and I instantly reach over and turn the oven off. Oh hell yeah, we can eat much later.

My eyes flip up and catch her nearly at the door of my bedroom. Completely naked from the waist up, that compass rose I inked between her shoulder blades looking all sexy on her perfect back. She glances over her shoulder at me and gives me a smile. I go after her, panting dog that I am, and catch her up in my arms just inside my bedroom. She squeals, but quickly sinks into me when I press her back against the door and kiss her. God damn, her skin feels like hot satin under my fingertips. I run them up her spine and groan when she shivers. I feel the heat off her pussy against my waist, and I want her. Now. Just get her in my bed and keep her there till we're both drunk on each other. But that's not the game we're playing. And I'm kinda dying to see her alone on the king size, legs spread, fingers doing what my aching dick wants to be doing.

With a pissed-off, hungry-as-fuck groan I release her and walk away, head for the chair near the bed. "Don't keep me waiting, Ads. I'm in no goddamn mood to wait."

Standing there in nothing but her tight jeans, her small waist v-ing upward to two handfuls of utter heaven, her eyes go kinda wide with surprise. Like maybe she didn't expect me to follow through on what I told her would happen when we got home. Like maybe she thinks I don't have the control. *Shit, baby, I barely do.*

"You want to see all of me, Rush?" she asks as she unbuttons, unzips and steps out of her jeans, nice and slow. I stare. Like the pig that I am. Her body's a fucking wonderland. Yeah, I know the song is bullshit, but it applies here. It applies to her. My baby. She's just all creamy skin, and dangerous curves my fingers are dying to wrap around and manipulate. But ultimately, it's the thong, that scrap of pink fabric she's removing as I stare with my fucking tongue hanging out of my head, that really makes my dick weep.

The thing is soaking wet.

My mouth waters and I lean forward in my chair. She's naked now. Just the way I like her. Well, naked and on top of me, or under me, or straddling my face.

"Lie down, baby." My voice is pretty gruff, but I'm running on fumes here. Don't know if I can make it through the entire peep show without coming in my pants. But hell, I'm going to try.

"All alone?" she asks, puffing out her lower lip enticingly.

I nod. "And all the way back to the pillows. But your eyes stay on me, yeah?"

"Always." She smiles at me. Sexy and sorta innocent too. She climbs onto the bed, and very slowly starts crawling on all fours toward the pillows.

My cock screams at me. I don't know how but the thing can see her, can see her ass and the pink, glistening lips of her pussy. It's torture. The sweetest kind around. When she turns and lies back against the pillows, her nipples are as hard as my dick, and my mouth is fucking begging me to just shut this stupid game down already. Fly at her and bury my head between her legs until tomorrow. Instead, I rip at the button of my jeans and yank my zipper down.

Her eyes drop, and when she catches sight of my cock she licks her lips. *Damn girl, why you gotta do that?*

"Now what?" she asks, knowing full well how insane she's making me, and loving it.

"Spread your legs, baby." My nostrils flare as I try to smell her. "Yeah, that's right. Let your knees fall to the side. Let me see you."

She does everything I ask, her eyes never leaving mine. She's bold, this girl. It's one of the many things that drive me wild about her. She's got balls, no fear, no embarrassment with me about her body or going as far as either of us want to.

"I want your tight, pink tits in my mouth, Addison," I say, letting my dick spring free, knowing come is leaking from the head and not

giving a shit. "Show me. Use your fingers and show me what my tongue would do to you."

She groans as she brings her hands to her breasts, squeezing, massaging, then pulling back to pinch the tips. Fuck, I'm dying here. I'm trying to act cool, like a badass, but all I want to do is devour her.

"Now take one hand," I tell her a little roughly. "And slide it down between your legs. Put two lucky fingers inside yourself and feel how wet you are."

Her eyes close as she runs her hand down her flat belly to her shaved pussy. Christ. I lick my bottom lip, bite the fucker, anything to keep myself in check. I'm going to be having motherfucking wet dreams for months after this. I don't want to be sitting here. I want to be licking at her, sucking on that swollen clit she's showing off.

I watch as her middle and index fingers slide between her wet lips, then disappear into her sex. She moans and not only spreads her legs wider, but lifts her knees to her chest.

"Fuck, Ads," I breathe.

She opens her eyes and pins me to my chair with the hottest, hungriest look ever. My heart is jacking against my chest, pre-come all over the head of my dick.

I growl out the words. "Now taste."

She stops, her fingers so deep inside of her, it's nothing but knuckles. "What?" she asks breathlessly.

"You heard me." I stand up, cock out, and move to the edge of the bed. "Take your fingers out of your pussy and put them in your mouth."

I watch, insane, as she does exactly what I say. But when her fingers leave her pussy and head for her mouth, when her juices coat the rim of her hungry, waiting lips, I'm done. I rip my clothes off, toss my boots at the wall so goddamn hard I'm pretty sure they make a mark. Then I lean across the bed, grab Addison by the hips and yank her to me. I'm on my knees just as her tight, hot pussy reaches my face. I use my thumbs to spread her wide, then lap her up like ice cream. She tastes like fucking sunshine and I devour her. I know it might be too fast or too hungry, but I can't help myself. As she writhes and humps my mouth, I suck on her clit, then flick it with my tongue. When I feel her tense,

63

feel her getting close to coming, I ease up a little, flatten my tongue against her ridge, and just let her ride me.

And motherfucker, she does. Crying out, crying my name, she bucks and rubs herself against my mouth and chin, and comes.

"Rush!"

"Already here, baby." I'm up and over her, pushing us both back on the bed. My thigh spreads her knees wider, and I slide into her tight, wet pussy and groan. She's still coming and my dick swells with the extra attention.

Positioned deep inside of her, I balance on my elbows for a sec and look down into her sick beautiful face. Those eyes…the green one that nearly matches my own—the one that belongs to

me. Seriously, this girl is mine. She's gotta be. There's no going back. Just forward.

"I love you, Ads. You know that right?"

Her eyes shift between heat and softness, and she nods. "Course I do."

"You happy here? With me?"

"Yeah. Always."

Something stabs me in the heart, some kind of warning or fear. I don't like the two-word answers. It's so not her. Why isn't she telling me she loves me back? Again, not her. And why does she look all uncomfortable answering my questions? What the fuck…

I groan because she's moving beneath me now, stealing my brain, bitch-slapping my concern. And well, shit, I'm only human. And a dude. And her body is my goddamn wonderland.

"God, you feel so good," she utters hoarsely, raking her nails up my back. "You make me feel so good, so happy."

It's enough for me. It's something. And when she wraps her legs around my waist, I kiss her, hard and deep. Just like my thrusts. My hands get tangled in her hair, and for minutes, hours, who the fuck knows, we just pump each other and say naughty shit that makes us laugh, but gets us off, too. It goes on like that until we both come. Then, like always, we wrap ourselves around each other and stop talking altogether. Cause it's off to dreamland, folks.

Addison

I'm completely disoriented when I wake up. At first I think I'm back in my apartment in Santa Barbara. Then my eyes adjust to the weak morning light filtering in through the windows, and my skin registers the warm, hard muscle against me. I shift in his arms, careful not to wake him, and rest my cheek and chin on my palm. This is kind of my thing, lying here in the morning and staring at him while he sleeps. Seriously, I know. I have issues. But he's so beautiful. Lying on his back, covers off, and I get to inspect every inch of him. From his feet, his hard calves and lean thighs, which are lightly sprinkled with hair, to his cock, which is at that halfway point to hardness I love so much. My mouth waters as I contemplate waking him up the old-fashioned way.

He stirs, and my gaze drifts to his hip bones. They rock my world, so bitable, so perfect to grip when I'm doing that old-fashioned wake-up thing. His stomach is truly six-pack heaven, covered in tongue-tracing ink, but not in a bodybuilder way. Just deliciously lean. And then, you know, there's the face. The face that caught me back when we were idiot kids, and the face that never left my memory bank when I fucked up and he bolted. Now it just makes me equally love him and hate him because I can never get enough of it.

Maybe I'll kiss him first. Just once. Those lips are calling to me. Then I'll head south. My gaze drops once again, but this time, instead of seeing where we are in the woody department, it comes to

a halt on his right hand. At first I'm not sure I'm seeing correctly. Or maybe I'm still asleep. My heart swells inside my chest a little as I follow the line work down his thumb. He's inked my name in his skin. He's inked my name into his skin? How didn't I see that yesterday?

Oh, I don't know, my brain razzes me. Maybe because you were acting like a lunatic. A sex-crazed lunatic who was desperately afraid her man would bolt if he knew how far over the moon for him she was.

Needing a moment to process, I slip out of bed and put on one of Rush's t-shirts. The sun is starting to rise for real now as I walk into the kitchen, and I stop for a second to bask in a particularly warm pool of it near the table. I love this room. It has killer light, and a view that makes you want to stare out the glass for hours. I check out things in the fridge, then follow an amazing scent to the oven. Ahhh, he had dinner waiting on us last night. Well, we're just a few hours late. No worries.

I start pulling stuff out and placing it on the already-set table. It's a pretty fancy to-do with all the crystal and copper and silver, and I feel kind of bad we didn't get to experience it with the moonlight streaking in, and that breeze he gets here.

He inked my name into his skin.

I hold on to the back of the chair and just say that again in my mind. *And* he told me he loved me. Clearly he wants me in his life for longer than a hot minute. So what's my problem? What's my fear?

Strong arms encircle my waist, and hard cock through thin cotton boxer briefs presses against my barely-covered ass. "Don't do me like that, Ads."

His breath on my neck sends tiny shards of heat straight to my well-worked-over bits.

"I have to wake up without you all week long. It fucking sucks."

"I know. I'm sorry."

He chuckles softly against my neck. "No apology needed, baby. Just a promise, all right? And you know I'll make it worth your while."

I smile, and those shards of heat turn all electric inside my pussy. I glance down, see his right hand splayed on my stomach. See my name there. For good. For always. The thing screams up at me. *The dude loves you, idiot. Stop with the cold play and tell him how you feel. Tell him just how crazy he makes you. How weak and vulnerable you feel when you guys aren't together.*

I sink back into him, gently grind my ass against his dick.

"Awwww, damn," he says on a quick intake of breath. "Can't. Fucking want to so bad. But can't." He turns me around and kisses me hard and hungry. When he pulls back, he looks like a sullen teenager. "I have a short day today at the shop, but I have to go in early."

I give him my most seductive look, which is really just a sort of pout-plus-eyelash-batting thing. I'm pretty sure it's not very effective. "You sure?"

He kisses my nose. "We have a guest artist. She's booked all day, and I need to open up and do the owner thing."

"Does she do tats?"

"Piercings."

"Oh. I might like that. Maybe my nose or my eyebrow."

For a second, I swear I see a flicker of panic cross his features, but then I blink and it's gone. I chew my lip thoughtfully. "Course I do need to go on interviews after graduation. Maybe I should wait."

He nods. "You should always think through any changes to the body." His brows lift a fraction and he whispers, "Especially your body."

I reach down for his hand, the right one, and lift it up for us both to see. "Did you think this through, Rush?"

He doesn't look at it—his hand or my name. His eyes are locked to mine, and they're pretty heavy with affection. "Every damn day you weren't with me, baby."

This is it. The perfect moment, if that even exists. To tell him. Right now, while we're stuck together and our stomachs are making strange-ass noises because we haven't eaten since yesterday afternoon. But I don't want to rush things either. I know he's got to go. But—and this is really inside my head now—I also know he's coming back.

His hand still in mine, I lead him over to the table. "Sit down. You gotta eat before you go."

"Fine." He watches as I fill up his plate, then grabs a fork. But when he notices I don't take the seat beside him, he frowns. "Aren't you hungry, baby?"

I nod. "Starving."

"Then come."

As he stuffs a piece of naan into his mouth, I pull my t-shirt up over my head, then toss it

somewhere behind me. Fork in hand, Rush stares at me, watches me as I walk over to his chair and kneel down in front of him.

"The only one coming this morning is you," I say, slipping my fingers into the waistband of his black boxers and easing them down just enough so that I can take care of business.

As I wrap my fingers around his cock, I glance up at him. His nostrils are flared, and the veins in his neck, even under all that ink, are popping. But he's still holding the fork. I lean in and run my tongue from thick base to wet tip.

"Think you can do two things at once, Merrick?" I ask, then take him slow and deep into my mouth.

"Fuck," he groans as metal fork hits hardwood floor. "No."

RUSH

Erica Day is like a cross between Kat Von D and Scarlett O'Fucking Hara, and once upon a time I thought she might be the girl for me. We had a ton in common, same biz, same taste in music, good for a laugh. I even opened up to her a little. Told her about the girl who had owned me once upon a time, then shattered my heart. Told her about the vanilla asshole, the Campbells, the dance and how I ran off afterward. But instead of letting me just vent and offering a few 'She missed outs' Erica talked about it all the damn time. Questions, questions, questions. It drove me nuts. It drove me away. So needless to say, even though it's been three years,

I'm thinking that keeping her and Ads apart might be a good idea.

"I'm rocking a nipple piercing in five, ya'll," Erica twangs. "And no, Vincent, you can't go in and 'check that shit out.'"

Hanging out behind the front desk, I glance up from the books. V, Janie and Erica are all chill in the reception area. I got one more canvas and then I'm outie, off to be with my girl. Right now, Addison is driving around in one of my cars, picking up food for tonight. Said she wants to cook me dinner before she leaves, and I'm thinking that's going to be the perfect time to slip her my extra key and ask her if she'll move here and use it on a daily basis. I'm nervous as fuck she'll say no. She's got that whole life back in Cali. A place, a best friend,

maybe even a job hook-up. Will she be cool about starting over—no, starting fresh—here with me?

"Hey, Miss Day." V gets up from the couch and hustles over to me. He rolls his eyes. "I just offered to help. Sometimes a girl can use an extra pair of hands."

"True," Erica concedes, giving Janie a quick wink.

How such different chicks bonded so quickly, I'll never know. Janie is a hard-ass ink master with a 1950's style and legs completely covered in tats. Erica, on the other hand, is soft spoken, free of ink, a natural blond, and dresses like a conservative Southern belle, though we all know she's got about ten piercings underneath.

"And by the way, Miss Day," Vincent calls out to Erica, elbowing me in the ribs like he thinks he doesn't have my complete attention. "If it's possible, you're even hotter now than back when you were banging Rush."

Janie purses her ruby-red lips at him. "You're such a heathen, Vincent."

He nods, smirks. "Thanks."

"Oh, Vincent, you haven't changed," Erica says, then slides her brown gaze to me. "But what about our friend here? Rush Merrick. The tall, handsome, tatted-up and not-very-chatty owner of Wicked Ink. Has he changed since all that banging occurred?"

Vincent laughs. "Fuck yeah, he has."

Her pale brows drift up. "Really? How?"

"Dude's got a serious girlfriend."

Her casual back and forth gives way to a moment of actual interest. "Is that right, Rush?"

I nod.

"So true love has finally bitten you in the ass."

Her southern drawl is kind of grating on the old eardrums. Never noticed that before. "Not the ass, no."

Her eyes remain locked with mine. "Good. Glad to hear it, doll. You deserve it after that mess way back when." She winks. "See. I don't forget, honey."

"Forget what?" Vincent asks, looking from one of us to the other. "What mess?"

"V, you're drooling on the desk," Janie says, smoothing down that elaborate pin-up girl hairstyle she loves so much.

Vincent ignores her. "What happened? I need to know or I won't sleep tonight."

Janie laughs. "You're such an idiot, V."

"Don't pretend like you don't want to know, J," he returns with a faux sneer.

Ignoring them both, Erica asks me, "So, do I get to meet her?"

"Nope."

"Why's that, honey? She a jealous little kitten?"

I'm really trying to remember what the fuck I saw in this chick when the front door opens and a client walks through it. She's got a row of small rings through one eyebrow and both nostrils pierced. Halle-fucking-luyah.

I turn back to Erica. She's still watching me with way too much interest.

"Someone here to see you, Miss Day," I say with a touch of the gruff. "Don't want to keep her waiting."

Addison

Lisa: he kissed me

Me: and that's a problem?

Lisa: with only his tongue

Me: BARF

Lisa: I think I can still taste him

Me: when are u seeing him
again?

Lisa: nxt wk

Me: SRSLY?!?

Lisa: his bro is graduating w/us.

he'll be @ the ceremony. our fams

are having brunch (kill me now)

Me: well congrats

Lisa: on what?

Me: the engagement

Lisa: FUCK U

Me: hardy har har

Lisa: so…howzit going there? how r

all the tattooed bad boys n girls? I'm

sure they're doing all sorts of

improper shit. (sighs)

Me: come w/me next time & u

can see 4 yrself

Lisa: how's Rush?

Me: he tattooed my name on

his hand

Lisa: wtf?

Me: addison...right down his

thumb

Lisa: no shit?

Me: it's so hot. he's so hot.

Lisa: BARF.

Me: he told me loved me, Lis.

Lisa: course he did, beeyotch.

Me: I'm gonna talk 2 him

tonite. tell him everything

Lisa: good!

Me: I'm even @ grocery

store buying shit I can't

pronounce & wine from

sometime before 2013!

Lisa: fancy. just don't max yr credit

card

Me: k

Lisa: loves you, whore.

Me: back atch, beeyotch. and

hey, sry abt yer date

Lisa: (shrugs) maybe it'll b better the

2nd time. have fun tonight & I'll c u

when u land.

Me: k thx bye

RUSH

"This is so sick, man," my client says as we walk out of my room and into the recep area.

Everyone's gotta be working because the place is dead.

I pat my guy on the back. "Glad you like it, man." Dude's been on my waiting list for eighteen months, and even though I kinda wanted to blow him off today to hang with Addison, I'm not that big of a prick.

Before we hit the front door, he turns and shakes my hand. He's somewhere in his mid-sixties, and I love the fact that he's still totally into scoring ink. Especially with the process being a little trickier on older skin. But this badass didn't have to take a break once in four hours.

"It was so worth the wait," he tells me. "And the drive from New Mexico."

"Well, when you're ready for your next one, you let me know. I'll get you in. No more of this eighteen months shit."

"You got it. Thanks, brother." He tosses me a salute and heads out the door.

Hot damn. All done. Time to grab my keys and get home to my baby. V says he's gonna lock up, so there's a fifty percent shot it'll get done. No worries though. After I drop Ads at the airport I'll come back and check on things.

"Hey, Rush, man!" Vincent calls from the dungeon. "Come in here."

SHATTERED
ink

For about two seconds, I wonder if I can pretend I didn't hear him and get the hell out the door and on my way. Shit, Ads and I only have 'til midnight. I want to taste her grub, then taste her.

"Rush, I know you're out there," V calls again. "Get your ass in here."

Fuck. Fine. Thirty seconds. That's all he gets. I head for his room. The kid always keeps his door open. It's policy for him. He tells his clients he's agoraphobic, but that's total bullshit. He likes to keep an eye on the door. Who's walking in. If she's hot. And if she's brought another hot chick with her for support.

"What do you want, V?" I say, coming up on his door. "I'm about to take off…"

I nearly hit the doorjamb with my face, because sitting in Vincent's chair, which incidentally is shaped like an electric chair, complete with restraining straps—*the douchebag had the thing custom made*—is my baby. Addison.

"What are you doing?" Even as the words come tumbling out of my mouth I have the answer. V's got his gloves on and Ads has her arm exposed. Holy shit.

"She asked me, man." Wiping some goo onto the inside of her forearm, V flashes me his pearlies. "And you know, I make it a policy to never say no to chicks who have hot asses."

"Oh, Vincent, you're such a charmer," Addison says dryly, though her eyes are on me. "How Lisa didn't see that in you, I'll never understand."

That shuts him up in a hurry. I gotta remember that trick for next time.

"How long have you been here?" I ask her, but my eyes are already traveling down her arm, over the script V's just put on her.

"Half hour," she says. "So…what do you think?"

I scratch my head, staring at it. What *do* I think? My name on her body. *RUSH* in black ink. Fuck me hard, it's what I wanted. It makes my insides all warm and shit, and my mouth hungry to kiss her. But then there's something else snaking around in there. Down low in my gut.

"Rush?"

I look up. Addison is staring at me, sorta excited and worried all at the same time. "You okay?"

LAURA WRIGHT

"Hey, ya'll," comes a southern singsong from the door. It fuses with that thing snaking around in my belly and puts me in an instant bad mood.

"I wouldn't normally do this," she keeps on. "But my client wants to show it off."

Vincent's head jerks around so fast I'm pretty sure he's gonna be dealing with whiplash later. "Who wants to show what off?"

"My sweet little client has just had a clit piercing."

Vincent makes a noise like air being let out of a balloon. It makes Addison laugh.

"Rush can finish me up, V," she says, looking up at me. "After all, this part of my skin belongs to him now. And you know, that clit thing sounds like a can't-miss event."

"Shit, man," Vincent says to me, pulling off his gloves and stuffing them in the trash. "You managed to score the coolest chick on the motherfucking planet, you know that?"

"Oh, he knows," Addison says. "Don't you, baby?"

It's pretty useless to try and stop something that's just fucking inevitable. But I do. For a second, I actually attempt to send Erica a mental email. Message Line: *Get the fuck out and don't say shit to Addison.* But you know. Useless. She strolls into the room and comes over to where we're all hanging out.

"So this is your girlfriend, Rush?" Her eyes are moving over Addison like she's a freaking painting to be studied, maybe even interpreted.

Fuck. There's nothing to do, but do. "Erica Day this is Addison Cramer."

"Hey," Ads says, offering her hand. "It's nice to meet you."

Erica shakes it, but it's super chill, kinda that up-and-down-once-and-we're-done thing. "Addison?"

Oh, hell.

Ads nods. "Yeah. And let me say, I think it's so cool what you do. Maybe when you come back again you could squeeze me in?" She stops and laughs at herself. "Not for the clit thing, probably. You know. I should probably start small. Eyebrow or nose or nipple."

Addison is being cute as fuck and I just want to grab her out of V's electric chair and take her home.

But Erica has just tasted blood and she's clearly ready to go all vampire on us.

"Wait," she starts, turning to me. "Wasn't that ex-girlfriend from high school, the one who stepped out with some other guy and broke your heart, named Addison?"

I don't answer her. But I'm pretty sure she sees and understands the death stare I'm throwing her way. We are no longer friends, or colleagues.

"That's some coincidence," she adds.

Hearing our history laid bare by a stranger has Addison up out of her chair. Gone is the cute as fuck thing. Her eyes are pinned to Erica. "How do you know about that?"

Erica shrugs innocently. "Rush told me. Back when we were together."

"Together?" Addison repeats, then looks over at me.

"Yeah," she said. "It really tore him up. Really affected the way he communicated. Our sex life was—"

"Okay, that's enough," I say in the coldest voice imaginable. "Erica, you have a pierced clit waiting on you and a full day of appointments. I suggest you get the fuck on it. And then after that, get the fuck out."

For a moment, she has the decency to look contrite. "I'm sorry, honey. That was out of line. I just kinda wanted to know." She shrugs, gives me one last tight smile, then leaves the room.

When I look back, Addison is standing by V's table and taping up her arm.

I go over to her and reach for her hand. "Let me do that."

She pulls away from me. "So, is this why you sort of discouraged me from coming in today?"

I'm not about to bullshit her. "Yeah."

She looks up. "Why?"

"Come on, Ads. She was three years ago. I don't give a fuck about her. But I do give a fuck about you. I didn't want you to feel uncomfortable."

"No. You didn't want *you* to feel uncomfortable."

"She's a pain in the ass. Clearly loves causing trouble. She knew about what happened back in high school and I didn't want you to hear that."

"But I did hear about it," she returns hotly.

"Only because you came here."

Her mouth drops open an inch.

"Shit." I growl at my foot-in-mouth assholery. "That's not what I mean. I'm glad you're here. I want you here all the damn time. I just didn't want you to have to deal with that kind of drama."

She lifts her chin, her nostrils flaring now. She's super pissed. "I suspect that being with you, I'm going to be exposed to all kinds of drama. I know you haven't been celibate since high school, and I know what kind of tail comes through that door several times a day. Stop protecting me, and prepare me."

"What?"

"I could've handled that bitch. But you didn't prepare me." She tosses the rest of the tape on the table and heads for the door. "I'm out of here."

I follow. Course I fucking follow. I love her to death. "Addison."

SHATTERED
ink

"I need some time, Rush." She doesn't even slow, doesn't even glance over her shoulder. Just hits the front door of the shop and keeps on going.

Once outside, I stop. She's already in my car, and she's right. I fucked up. She deserves some cooling off. Shit. This was not the day I had planned.

Without looking at me, Addison backs up and drives off.

After a minute of staring at her receding taillights, I head back inside. I'm feeling murderous and I'm ready to fire anyone who crosses my path and says something stupid.

Vincent's behind the desk, taking a credit card from his client. "She gone?" he asks.

I shoot him a warning glare. "What do you think?

"I told you, man," he says with exactly zero

sympathy. "Name tats. Kiss of fucking death."

Addison

I lift the wooden spoon to my mouth and taste. Holy crap, that's some kickass gravy. I stare into the pot. It looks good. Brown and bubbling and sending off hella good scents. I'm kind of proud of myself. Coq au Vin had sounded super difficult and majorly time consuming, and yeah, it was both those things, but I did it.

I'm just taking another quick taste, when I hear the front door open. My pulse jacks up in my throat, but I'm glad he's home. And I'm appreciative of the hour he's given me to cool down.

"You're making dinner, Ads?"

I turn to look at him. "I told you I was going to."

He's leaning against the counter about five feet away. "I know, but I thought…" His body language is wary, but his eyes are throwing off hardcore forgive-me darts. God, I'm so in love with him.

"Did you think I'd be on my way to the airport, Rush?"

He nods, and I hate the flash of fear in his eyes.

"Oh, Jesus." I put the spoon down and lean against the counter, too. "I'm not running from this. I fucking love you. It took us five years to get here."

His eyes close and he exhales. "Oh, Ads."

When he opens them again, I continue, "But you can't lie to me. No matter what. No matter how you think I'm going to react." My words catch up with me and sucker punch me in the chest. I laugh

softly. At myself. My silly, fearful, happy self. "Amazing."

"What?"

"I learned something from this. From that asshole ex of yours. Seriously, she might be from the south or whatever, but girl needs to learn some manners."

Rush pushes away from the counter and saunters over to me. And when I say 'saunters,' I mean it. Boy may be scared of losing what we got, but nothing can steal his sexy.

"You gotta know something," I say when he places his hands on my hips and pins me with those jade-green eyes. "And if it sends you running out the door, then fine, I get that. Of course, this is your house so maybe I'm the one who leaves, or you step out for a walk and…"

His hands tighten around my hips and he eases me closer. "Ads. Talk to me. I'm not going anywhere."

I take a breath, bite my lower lip. "Okay. Here goes. So, I've been in hell for five weeks."

His body goes rigid. "What?"

"Except when I'm with you," I amend quickly. "When I'm with you I'm crazy happy. Like, nuts happy. Like I can breathe and chill and focus. But when I'm back there, when I'm home, without you, life just completely sucks. Seriously, it's orange sweatpants and sad movies, pining all night instead of studying, and being an utterly craptastic friend. I'm lost." I shrug. "I'm addicted. To you. To us."

"See, that's the problem, baby," Rush says casually, like all the shit I just said was completely and totally understandable.

"What?" I ask. I think my Coq au Vin might be burning. And I think I don't care.

"Cali's not your home."

I swallow. No. Definitely don't care about the fancy French chicken. "It's not?"

He shakes his head. "Come on, Addison. We're both shit without each other. Phone's not going to do it. Text just pisses me off. And weekends are a goddamn tease."

I nod, laugh. "I know, totally."

He pulls back a second, his brows slamming together. He looks so hot when he's confused. "Wait a minute. Did you actually think I'd be freaked out or turned off by hearing how sick your love for me is?"

"Yeah. I kinda did." I shake my head. "That abandonment thing runs deep, you know? And when you find that person who just drives you crazy in the freaking best way, like they get you, and all you want to do is be with them, you get scared. You get scared 'cause you wanna hang on tight. Crazy tight. And you wonder if you'll suffocate them and they'll break away and haul ass to a different state or country or…the moon." I start laughing at myself. I'm such a nutjob.

Rush pulls me in for a kiss. It's not the hungry, I'm-going-to-fuck-the-shit-out-of-you kind, which is pretty standard for us because we're horny and in love. It's gentle and vulnerable, and it makes tears prick in my eyes.

When he pulls away, there's something near my cheek. I can't see it because it's out of my eyeline, but I think it's metal. Then he brings it around and holds it between us.

"Move in and suffocate the shit out of me, Ads. And before you say anything, that's not a question." He takes the key and heads for the top of my tank. I gasp when he places the cool metal between my breasts. His eyes lift to hold mine. "I was going for your heart, but I'm not that skilled in the romantic notions department."

I wrap my arms around his neck and get as close as possible. "Oh, I think you're pretty good."

"And I think you're pretty."

I giggle like a girl. "Maybe we should turn off the stove?"

"Definitely."

He flips the switch in one easy movement, then hauls me into his arms and kisses me again. And this time, it's totally hungry and I-want-to-fuck-the-

111

shit-out-of-you. And you know what? We can eat

later.

Lisa

My mom cups my face and stares at me with tears in her eyes. "You looked so beautiful up there, darling. I'm so proud of you."

"Thanks, Mom."

It's crazy time. All around us, graduates in caps and gowns are celebrating. Some with their families, some with their friends.

"Now, if they'd have just allowed you to wear something other than black."

I ease away from her hold. "Mom—"

"It's just so drab, darling." She lowers her voice. "And Kevin was watching."

"You think Kevin would prefer me in…pink, purple?"

She lifts one perfectly penciled brow. "Don't be a shit, darling."

I laugh. At just that moment, my father, Kevin and his parents join us. Mr. and Mrs. Stanfield are pretty much a carbon copy of my parents. Tan, toned, aging beautifully, dressed in tailored pastels. It's the world I grew up in, and honestly—and sadly—the world I feel most comfortable in. But I try as best I can to venture out and be bad. I think I've succeeded a few times.

My dad scoops me up in his arms and swings me around like I'm six. "My little college graduate." He places me down and glances over at the Stanfields. "They grow up so fast. Leave the nest and fly off for parts unknown."

I laugh. "Dad, I'm not flying off. Not until I find a job that sends me places."

SHATTERED
ink

"A job," my mother says, clucking her tongue and fingering her pearls. "You don't have to worry about that."

"I'm not worried," I lie. "I'm ready."

My mother's steely gaze drifts over to Kevin, who is looking at me with soft affection. I cringe. The last thing in the world I want is another date with The Tongue.

"You know, I was already married with a baby on the way when I was your age, Lisa." My mother touches the sleeve of Kevin's ultra-pressed white shirt. "Do you like children, Kevin?"

He looks momentarily startled, so his mother answers for him. "Adores them."

Oh, Jesus. I need to get to an after-party, like now. Before they start planning our wedding.

"Brunch at the Biltmore, Meredith?" my father asks.

She nods. "Yes. We have reservations for one o'clock."

"Then we'd better get going." My father turns to me. "Why don't you ride with Kevin, honey? We old folk like to stick together." He gives me a wink.

Real subtle, Dad.

"I brought the Porsche today," Kevin says, moving closer to me. "I remember you how much you like it. The seats especially." His eyebrows drift up and down a couple times in an effort to be provocative.

Real subtle, Kev.

He tries to put his arm around me, but I feint right. I seriously can't bear him touching me again.

116

Just the memory of his tongue coming at me like a knight's lance, ready to do battle. BARF.

He's so not deterred. "After brunch we can take it for a ride on the beach. I know a strip of sand that's totally abandoned. Maybe there's a few animals around, but I can get them out of my way. Permanently, if you know what I mean."

I do. I really do. I stare at his shirt and all the buttons. I really do hate buttons.

"Hey, girl!" Someone jumps me from behind, then whispers in my ear, "What's up, whore?"

Oh, thank god.

"Addy, where have you been?" I say, turning around to verbally flog her for not being by my side as my parents attempt to marry me off to Mega Buttons. But she's not alone. And I very much mean NOT ALONE.

I eye the two guys dressed completely out of place for a morning graduation ceremony in Santa Barbara. Jeans and t-shirts and lots of ink. "Hey, Rush. Vincent."

Now, I knew Addison's man was coming to the ceremony, obviously, but I had not been informed that she had also invited his jerkoff friend.

"Well, Lisa dear," my mother says behind me. "Are you going to introduce us to your…friends?"

Oh, yeah, sure. This won't be awkward. "Mom, Dad, Mrs. and Mrs. Stanfield, Kevin, you know my best friend, Addison." I wait for the little nods between them all to cease before I continue. "And this is her boyfriend, Rush. And this is…" *The hottest guy that ever walked the earth.* No. That's not right. I'm flustered. "This is…" *The guy who*

SHATTERED
ink

once—oh, god. No, No, No... "This is one of Rush's employees, Vincent." Better. But not much.

Addison's looking at me like I'm having a stroke or something. Rush is shaking hands with my parents and Mr. and Mrs. Stanfield. And Vincent, with his 'Suck Me Raw' t-shirt and nearly shaved skull, is just staring at Kevin like he's about to bust out laughing.

"You both have some nice artwork there," Kevin says politely, first pointing at Rush's neck, then at Vincent's sleeve tattoo—the one with *pussy wagon* scrawled down the forearm.

"Thanks, man," Rush says.

"Yeah, thanks," Vincent says like he means the exact opposite. "Hey, if you're ever in Vegas, come by. I can hook you up."

"For a tattoo?" Kevin says, surprised and slightly uncomfortable. "Oh. Yeah, I don't know. Maybe."

"A pin-up with a skull face would look really sharp on your neck."

Someone clears their throat behind me.

"My son will not be getting a tattoo," Mrs. Stanfield says sharply. "He's going to law school."

"Right." Vincent's gaze flickers to me. "No blue ink for the blue blood."

"Lisa?" my father begins. "What is he talking about?"

I turn and death-stare at Vincent. "I have no idea," I utter through gritted teeth.

His lips drift upward. "Yeah you do."

"V," Rush says under his breath. "Don't."

Vincent's gaze flickers over to Kevin, then back to me. "Perfect. Your own kind, Lis. It's where you belong."

"Shall we go? *On y va?*" my mom purrs in her I've-been-to-Paris-more-times-than-you-can-count French accent. "Brunch awaits."

I roll my eyes. Good to know Vincent isn't the only asshole in this crowd.

"It was lovely to meet you all," my mother says. But her tone pretty much says the opposite.

"You too," Addison says quickly, giving me the most heartfelt I'm-sooooooo-sorry look.

She pulls both boys away by their offensive t-shirts, but not before Vincent gives me the biggest shit-eating grin on the planet. For one second, I stare after him. Black jeans, fine ass, broad shoulders, sleeves of tattoos, and the words *Bite Me* shaved into the back of his head.

I turn back to Kevin. He's smiling at me and holding up the keys to his Porsche.

Fuck, I hate buttons.

The End

NEW YORK TIMES BESTSELLING AUTHOR
LAURA WRIGHT

COMING

MAY 18, 2015

REBEL
ink

WICKED INK CHRONICLES

SHAMELESS

MASTERS OF SEDUCTION

SERIES

CHAPTER ONE

Fire licked at Rosamund's ankles. Wet, rough, fire that moved tantalizingly up her calves to her knees, then slowed as it settled between her thighs. A groan of desire escaped her throat. But she did nothing to try and quell it.

She needed this.

Him.

Like one needed air and water.

"Rosamund, wake up…"

The words were a distant whisper. Unwelcome. Irritating. She pushed them away and focused on the man before her. He was poised over her sex now, spreading her thighs wide with his long, thick fingers, his insistent palms. Though her eyes were closed, she could see him. Fierce, hungry, his smile invitingly wicked.

"Is she ill?" It was another voice now, once again female and worried.

"No, no," came the first voice, her tone threaded with false concern. "She is still sleeping. Poor, sweet Rosamund. Perhaps she is dreaming of what she can never have."

The man's smile morphed into something sexually sinister, and Rosamund's insides went instantly liquid.

"Don't be cruel, Eva," said the second female.

"It is not cruel to speak the truth," the first female returned, her voice slightly muffled.

"If she would just allow us to see to her. Bathe her. Rub her skin with salts and oils. Do her hair.

Dress her. Perhaps one of the males would notice her."

Rosamund's heart beat furiously against her ribs. Gone was the male's gaze. *Oh yes*! His head was between her trembling thighs now. She lifted her hips in anticipation.

"You say this as though it would be the easiest task in the world," answered Eva. "One cannot turn a tuft of esparto grass into a rock rose no matter the efforts."

"She is tall and slender, and has beautiful eyes."

"Indeed," Eva conceded. "Like the golden desert sands. But her face and teeth, hair and posture…"

Rosamund gasped as the man ran his nose along the seam of her sex. Why couldn't they go away? These stupid, silly Nephilim? Their opinions meant nothing to her. All she wanted was this male. His mouth on her. His tongue inside her.

"Rosamund, you must wake!" called the second female, more urgently this time. "Constance is on her way. There is to be an announcement."

Rosamund drove her fingers into thick, soft hair in response. *Yes! Yes*! *Right there, male,* she urged, squeezing his scalp. He groaned, the sound vibrating against her heat as he nuzzled his way to her swelling clitoris.

The sound of a doorknob rattling entered her consciousness, but she pushed it away. It was the click of a lock being breached that truly yanked her from the rising pleasure, cutting into her dream like a guillotine to the neck. She came awake with a start, eyes flying open, body jackknifing upward into a sitting position. Breathing heavy, she glanced around, blinked. It was pitch black in her little anteroom—the space she'd claimed when she arrived in the Harem nearly one year ago. The space that was all hers. Every other Nephilim in residence lived in shared accommodations—very gratefully and happily. But Rosamund had wanted to be alone.

No. She'd needed to be alone.

"Rosamund, Constance will give you a week in the kitchens if you're not in attendance," Eva persisted, inching the door open.

Panic seized Rosamund. She couldn't have them see her. Not like this. "I'm up," she called, scrambling off her pallet and rushing to the door. She pressed herself against it, blocking their entrance. "I'm up. I'll be out in a few minutes."

There was a momentary pause, then a sigh. "All right," Eva said. "We will see you in the courtyard. And Rosamund?"

"Yes?" she said with a touch of irritation she wasn't quite awake enough to hide. Sleep still clung to her mind. Wet heat still claimed everything south of her navel.

"Good morning to you," the female called.

Oh great Goddess, it had been, Rosamund thought with a groan as she listened to the females' retreating footsteps. *Or could have been.* She heaved a sigh and let her head fall back against the wood. She was truly dying to know how her dream ended. She'd been having it nearly every night of her three hundred and sixty one nights in the Harem. And each time, the intensity grew, the need intensified. Granted, she could never see the male's face clearly, but she knew it was Roger. The human man she'd met and fallen for three months before she'd been called to the Harem. The human man who believed she was away on a yearlong animal research trip in the Australian bush.

The human man who had held her in his arms the night before she left and sworn that he would wait for her forever. But Rosamund knew forever was a relative term—and that waiting wasn't easy for anyone. Normally a letter from him came once a week, forwarded from a post office box in Sydney. But in the past couple of months she'd received nothing at all.

Her heart squeezed as she pushed away from the door. Just four more days, she reminded herself, setting about lighting the three lamps that lined her tiny bookcase and clothing rack. Four more days until she was back in San Francisco, back to Roger—back to creating the life, the home, the family, she'd always dreamt of having.

With quick, seasoned hands, she performed her daily routine. Tying down her breasts and padding her middle. Applying powders to her face to make her appear sallow and tired, and oils to her long, pale blond hair to make it appear unwashed. And the one last accompaniment that was a guarantee to her continued success—the one she'd had made before leaving San Francisco nearly a year ago—a dental prosthetic that made her teeth look almost rotten.

After slipping on the large pumpkin-colored day robe, she made a quick inventory of her appearance in the cracked half mirror. She looked as she did every day. A younger version of the witch who'd sold Snow White her poisoned apple. She heaved a great sigh of relief. Perfect. No male on Earth would choose her over the stunning Nephilim females of the Harem.

After turning off the lights, Rosamund exited her converted closet and headed down the flagstone hallway toward the courtyard. A cool, salty breeze from the sea nearly five miles south lapped over her heated skin. She groaned at the sensation. Would Roger come to her again tonight? Would he finally take her to completion? Or was he to ever torment her until she returned to him?

Sand surrounded the sumptuous Moroccan palace that had been the Harem of the Nephilim, and neutral ground to both Nephilim and Incubi, for centuries. But inside its sandstone walls, lush, fragrant gardens and pools carved out of rock reined. As Rosamund came into the courtyard, brilliant sunlight assaulting her vision, she saw that one of those pools was occupied. Ten or so Nephilim were swimming and splashing about, naked and bronzed and laughing gaily. Rosamund felt a pang of envy, of loneliness, in her heart. It was the same every day. Relaxing in the sun or the pools, dining on all sorts of lovely concoctions as the eunuchs fanned their heated skin. Friendships were being created out of leisure and decadence, and a shared understanding that being called up to the Harem by the Three was a great honor. One almost every female hoped would end in a full womb and a healthy baby.

Rosamund heard her name being called and turned to see Eva waving at her. The young and very beautiful redhead was standing with a group of three Nephilim who were gazing up at a marble statue of Demeter, the goddess of fertility. The statue was positioned on a small raised dais to the right of the rock pool. Rosamund hunched her shoulders and started forward in a slow, awkward manner befitting someone with an ever-present backache. As usual, a few females glanced her way and offered her a tight smile. Though they would never admit to it, they didn't like having her around. Not just because she didn't fit in with them socially, but because everything in the Harem was beautiful and seductive and immortal. And she reminded them that outside these walls ugliness and pain and mortality existed.

"I like that color on you, Rosamund," Eva said, unconsciously running her hand over the silk skirt of her lovely, formfitting blue takchita.

Rosamund smiled. "Thank you."

Facing the rotten teeth up close, the beautiful Nephilim blanched and turned away—just in time to see an attractive older female with thick dark hair knotted at the top of her head walk into the courtyard and over to the dais. She was flanked by two eunuchs, who wore serious expressions and little else. She climbed the four steps, stood in the center of the dais and called to the group of thirty, "Good morning, Nephilim."

Laughter died down and chatter ceased as every female turned to give the woman her attention.

"For the next two nights, we welcome a most honored guest." Her black eyes glittered with excitement and a broad smile curved her full lips. "The Incubus I speak of has not been to our Harem in nearly five years."

A few startled gasps rent the desert air. It was unheard of for an Incubus to go longer than a few months without visiting the Harem. Unless they were bonded to a female, of course. Though they could engage in sex elsewhere, pull their power elsewhere, the Harem was purported to give an Incubus the ultimate power surge.

"He is of most ancient blood," Constance continued. "And a strong, decided personality." Her black eyes moved over the crowd. "I have been told that unlike most of his Incubi brethren, there will be little preamble. No introductions. No voicing your interest. He will simply look on each of you and make his decision."

How strange, Rosamund mused. Not that there was a great deal of chit chat between an Incubus and the Nephilim he wished to bed. But a touch of hands, a few words spoken, eye contact—these were always utilized. Except when it came to her, of course. Incubi didn't even notice her, much less try and touch her.

"Who is it, Constance?" a Nephilim named Anya called out from the edge of the rock pool. "Do not keep us in suspense."

The woman's chin lifted a fraction, and Rosamund noticed that her hands trembled slightly at her sides. "Scarus Vipera."

A wave of excited whispers moved on the air, through the crowd. Rosamund glanced from female to female. They were smiling, eyes wide and eager.

"The Master of the House of Vipera himself," Constance went on, her voice taking on a husky quality. "It would be a great honor to carry his seed." Her eyes once again moved over the crowd.

"I suggest you prepare yourselves. He will be here at sundown."

Rosamund watched as the woman and the two eunuchs moved down the dais steps and left the same way they'd come. Oh yes. She would prepare herself. Most carefully.

"I wonder who he will choose for his first night," called a petite, pale-eyed Nephilim who was climbing out of the pool.

"I hope it's me," replied her friend, who was still in the water, her large breasts bouncing on the surface.

The petite woman toweled off her wet, naked skin. "I hear tell he is the most handsome of all the Incubi."

"I hear he is the most dangerous," called Eva, who was still standing beside Rosamund.

"Barbaric is what I was told," replied the woman in the pool. "And stoic."

A tall, stunning Nephilim reclining on one of the outdoor chaises laughed. "And I hear he is the most shameless."

"Whatever do you mean by that, Cleo?" the petite woman asked, wrapping the towel around herself.

The woman's light blue eyes, expertly lined in kohl, flashed with heat. "Just that he cares little for modesty in his bed."

Feminine giggles and trills of anticipation erupted from the women. They could hardly wait to meet this male, lie beneath him. Rosamund didn't blame them. Once upon a time, she too had been excited to come to the Harem and be taken by one of the handsome and virile Incubi of the nine

Houses. But that was before she'd met Roger. Before she'd realized that she wanted to give herself and her womb—and her heart—to one male.

Leaving the gaiety and plans for dress and hair and scent behind, Rosamund headed out of the courtyard and back to her room. She didn't know Master Scarus Vipera, had never seen him, and didn't expect even a glance her way when he walked the line of exquisitely painted and perfumed Nephilim this eve. But she would take no chances. She would prepare herself, as Constance had suggested. Make herself even more hideous than usual.

Four days.

That was all she had left until she was back in Roger's capable and comforting arms.

It was the ancient clause—the one she had found after getting her call from the Three, the one no Nephilim had ever spoken of. Yes, a Nephilim remained at the Harem until she bore one child. In exchange, she was granted immortality for that time. But if she was not chosen by an Incubus in one year's time, she must leave. Rosamund wondered if the Three believed that an Incubus could tell that a female wasn't good stock, couldn't produce a healthy babe.

Whatever the reason for the clause, she was grateful.

In just four days, she would be on her way home. To America. To her tiny apartment over the veterinary clinic. To Roger. To a chance for a real life, a future, and the family she had always wanted.